M000042492

Special Delivery!

by Steven Banks
illustrated by Vince DePorter

Ready-to-Read

Simon Spotlight/Nickelodeon

New York   London   Toronto   Sydney

SpongeBob was eating breakfast
at the kitchen table.
"Gary, look!" he said to his snail.
"I can get a free toy if I mail in
one hundred box tops!"
"Meow," said Gary.

So SpongeBob sat down
and ate one hundred boxes of cereal!

When he was finished eating,
SpongeBob ran to the post office
to send away for the toy.
"Now all I have to do is
go home and wait,"
said SpongeBob.

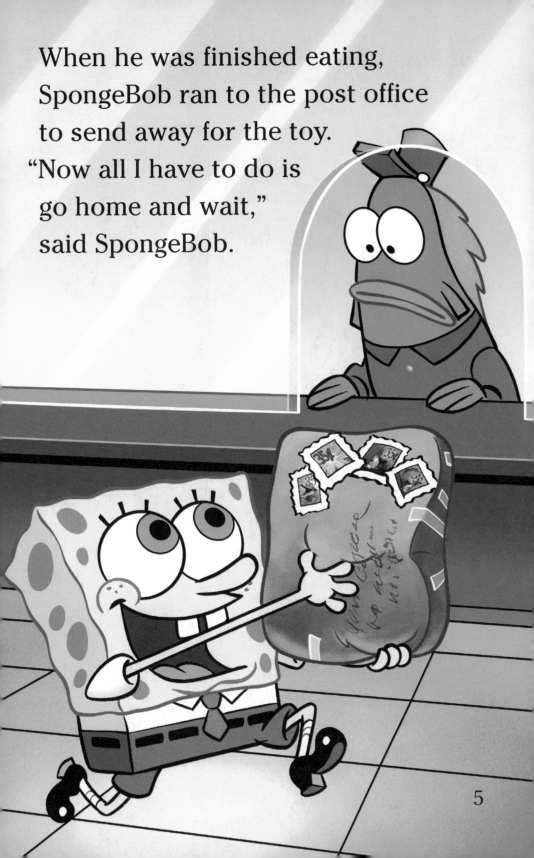

SpongeBob's best friend, Patrick,
came outside.
"What are you doing?" he asked.
"I am waiting!" said SpongeBob.

"Oh, boy!" cried Patrick.
"Can I wait too?"
"Sure!" replied SpongeBob.

SpongeBob and Patrick
waited by the mailbox.
"It's fun to wait!" said Patrick.
"It sure is!" agreed SpongeBob.

The next morning
Squidward saw SpongeBob and
Patrick waiting by the mailbox.
"What are you two doing out here?"
asked Squidward.
"We are waiting," replied Patrick.
"For what?" asked Squidward.
"I do not know!" said Patrick.

Squidward came outside.
"We are waiting for my free toy,"
explained SpongeBob.
"Oh, I thought we were waiting
for Santa Claus," said Patrick.

Just then the mailman walked up.
"Mr. Mailman, may I please
have my free toy?" asked SpongeBob.
"Are you crazy?" said the mailman.
"You just mailed in for it yesterday!"

Squidward looked at the cereal box.
"SpongeBob, it takes weeks for
your stupid toy to arrive!" he cried.

"Haven't we been waiting
   for weeks?" asked Patrick.
"You have only been out here
   for one night!" said Squidward.

"I will not leave this spot
until I get my toy!"
said SpongeBob.

"And I will stay by your side!"
said his loyal friend Patrick.
"We have not yet begun to wait!"
cried SpongeBob.

SpongeBob and Patrick waited.

And they waited.

Then they waited some more.

And they kept on waiting!

And then one day the mailman said,
"Here's your free toy."
"At last!" cried SpongeBob.
"I knew it would come!"
"And it got here so quickly!"
Patrick added.

"Open it! Open it!" cried Patrick.
"Wait," said SpongeBob.
"Let's go tell Squidward it's here.
He will not want to miss this!"
They ran to Squidward's house.

Squidward was practicing his
clarinet in the bathtub.
"Hey, Squidward, I got my free toy!"
said SpongeBob.
"Do you want to see it?"
"No!" said Squidward.
"But I am sure you will
show it to me anyway."

SpongeBob opened the box carefully
and pulled out a piece of red string.
"Here it is!" cried SpongeBob.
"My amazing free toy!"

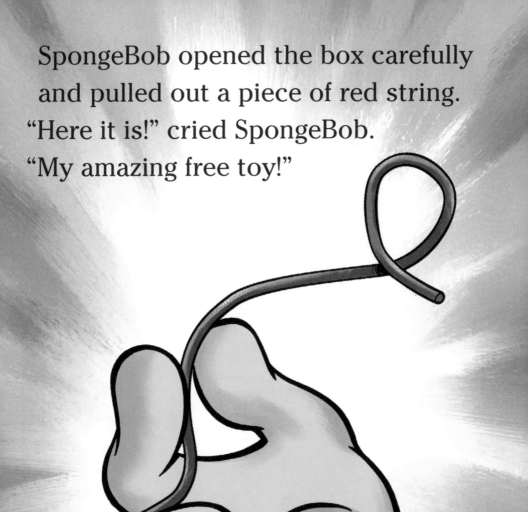

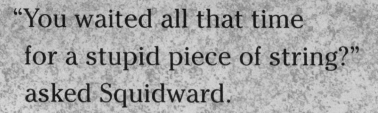

"You waited all that time
   for a stupid piece of string?"
   asked Squidward.
"Yes, but it's red! And it's free!
   And it's mine!" said SpongeBob.
   Squidward just shook his head,
   while SpongeBob ran around
   and played with his piece of string.

"Can I play with it?" asked Patrick.

"Okay, but be very careful,"
said SpongeBob.

"I waited a long time for this toy."

"You did?" asked Patrick.

As soon as he took the string,
it broke!

SpongeBob began to cry.
"My free toy! It's broken!"
"I am sorry, SpongeBob," said Patrick.
"It was an accident!"
"Serves you right
for wasting all that time
waiting for a cheap toy,"
said Squidward.

"He was a good little toy,"
SpongeBob said, sniffling.
"He was just too beautiful
for this cruel world.
Rest in pieces, little string."

Squidward looked out his window.
SpongeBob and Patrick were having
a service for the broken toy.
"Those losers," he said.
"Their crying is going to
keep me up all night!"

Squidward sneaked outside after dark
and dug up the little box.
"Thief!" cried SpongeBob
as Patrick shined his flashlight
on Squidward.
"Calm down, SpongeBob. It's just me,"
said Squidward.

Squidward took out the string
and tied the pieces together.
"See, it's as good as new."

"Squidward, you fixed it! You fixed
it for me!" cried SpongeBob.
"How can I ever thank you?"
"Just go home and be quiet!"
said Squidward as he
stomped back into his house.

"I know how we can thank him,"
SpongeBob told Patrick.
"We can send away for another toy!"
So they did, and they waited
right outside his window
for a long, long, long, long time!